D0461270

To e.E. Charlton-Trujillo, an incredible advocate and storyteller, and one of the bravest people I know —PZM

For my pal Kimberly Gee, the lightest and brightest —EW

ABOUT THIS BOOK: The illustrations for this book were done with India ink, watercolors, colored pastel pencils, and acrylic paint on Lanaquarelle Watercolor paper. This book was edited by Deirdre Jones and designed by Nicole Brown. The text was set in NicolasCocTOTReg, and the display type is handlettered. The production was supervised by Erika Schwartz, and the production editor was Annie McDonnell.

 • Little, Brown and Company • Hachette Book Group • 1290 Avenue of the Americas, New York, NY 10104 • Visit us at LBYR.com • First Edition: March 2019 • Little, Brown and Company is a division of Hachette Book Group, Inc. The Little, Brown name and logo are trademarks of Hachette Book Group, Inc. • The publisher is not responsible for websites (or their content) that are not owned by the publisher. • Library of Congress Cataloging-in-Publication Data • Names: Miller, Pat Zietlow, author. | Wheeler, Eliza, illustrator. • Title: When you are brave / by Pat Zietlow Miller ; illustrated by Eliza Wheeler. • Description: First edition. | New York : Little, Brown and Company, 2019. | Summary: Relates how to find your courage and use it when life seems scary or you start something new. • Identifiers: LCCN 2017043580| ISBN 9780316392525 (hardcover) | ISBN 9780316392495 (ebook) | ISBN 9780316392518 (library edition ebook) • Subjects: | CYAC: Courage—Fiction. • Classification: LCC PZ7.M63224 Wh 2019 | DDC [E]—dc23 • LC record available at https://lccn.loc.gov/2017043580 • ISBNs: 978-0-316-39252-5 (hardcover), 978-0-316-39249-5 (ebook), 978-0-316-44900-7 (ebook), 978-0-316-44901-4 (ebook) • PRINTED IN CHINA • APS • 10 9 8 7 6 5 4 3 2 1

When You Are BRAVE

By Pat Zietlow Miller
Illustrated by Eliza Wheeler

LB
Little, Brown and Company
New York Boston

Some days,
when everything around
you seems scary...

Brave as a bird that steps from its nest,
hoping to soar through the sky.

Brave as a dog that
wanders for miles,
searching for one
well-known light.

Brave as a caterpillar that builds a bed…

wondering when it will wake.

Because some days are full
of things you'd rather not do.

Like plunging into a
pool, all by yourself,
hoping you'll swim
and not sink.
Or standing alone,
in front of a crowd,
searching for one
friendly face.

Or boarding the bus and riding to school,
wondering what lies ahead.

At times like these, the world can seem…

Too big. Too loud. Too hard. Too much.

While you feel…
Too small.
Too quiet.
Too tired.
Not enough.

On those days, look deep inside to find the courage you need.

It might be hidden away, but…

If you close your eyes and
breathe, you will see it—
shining its light in the dark.
Warm. Steady. Safe.

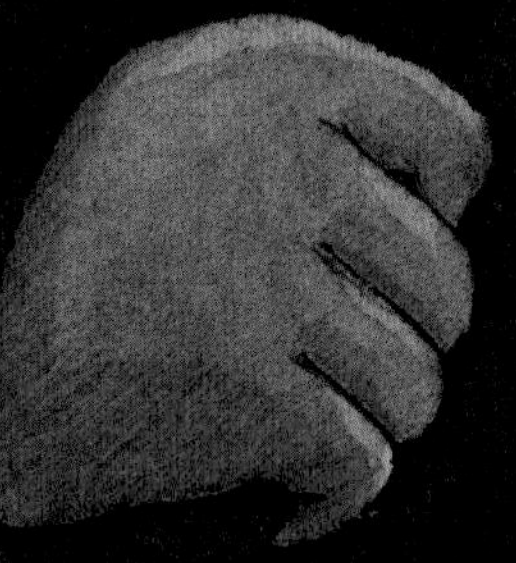

Your light might be small to start–just a spark–but you can turn it into a flame.

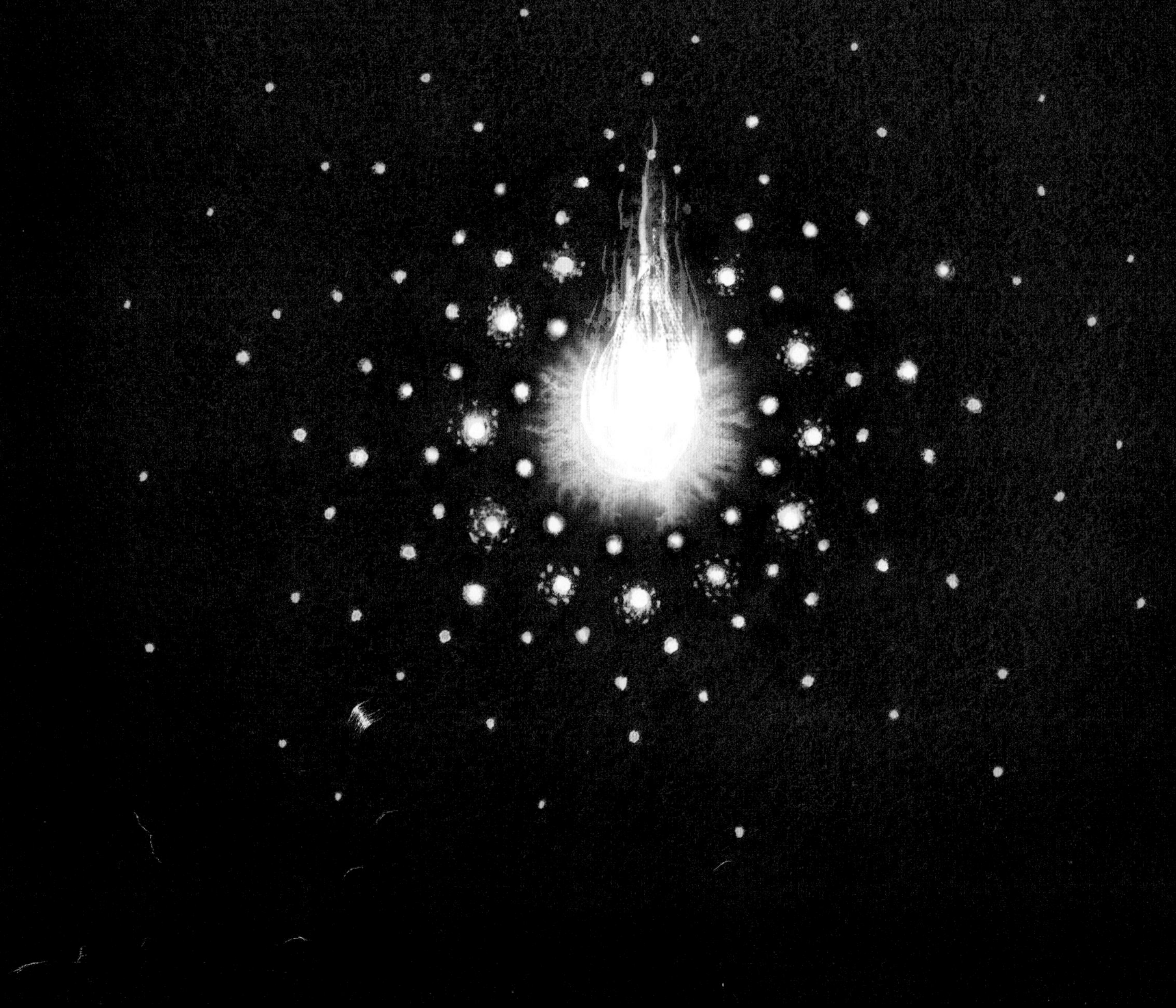

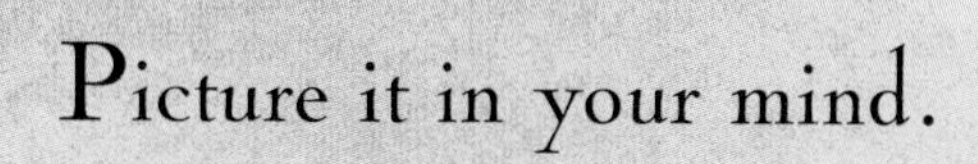

Picture it in your mind.

Then imagine it becoming
bigger and bolder.

You can make your courage
so big it brightens your heart,
fills your fingers, and flows to your toes.

Think about what you're good at.
Something you love.

Or someone
who loves you.

No one else will see it.
But you'll know you glow.

And you'll know you are ready.

No matter how deep the water,
how loud the crowd,
how hard the ride,
or how much there is to do.
You might struggle.
You might succeed.
People might clap.
Or laugh.
Or not notice at all.

No matter what happens,
you'll be all right.

Because once you find your courage, it's easy to use again and again.
The next time life seems scary or you start something new,
you can remember when you were brave.

And then, you can stand
straight and walk tall.

Knowing you are
as brave as…

a bird, a dog,
and a caterpillar.

As brave as...*you*.

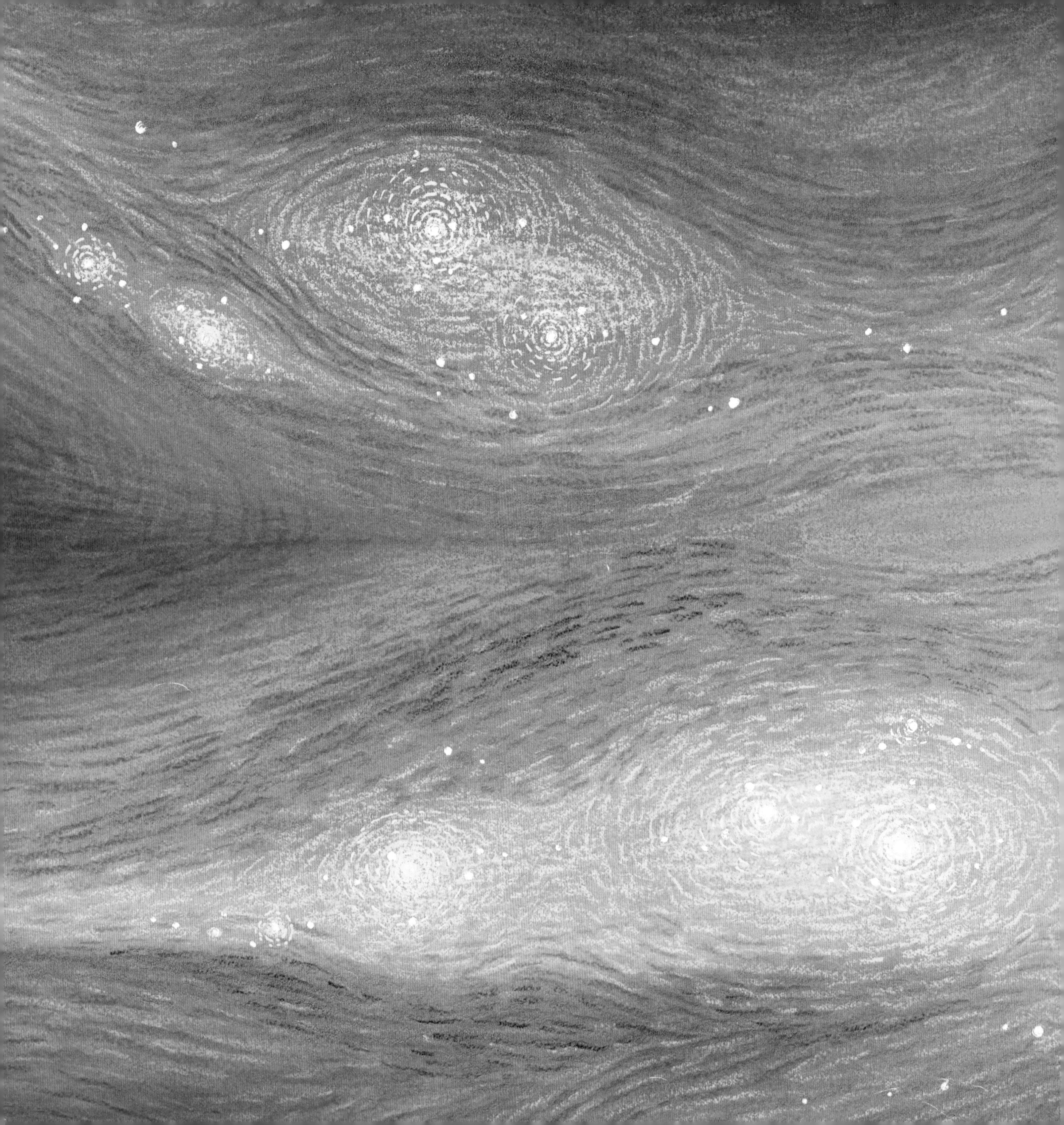